Dear Parents:

Congratulations! Your child is taking the first steps on an exciting journey. The destination? Independent reading!

STEP INTO READING® will help your child get there. The program offers five steps to reading success. Each step includes fun stories and colorful art or photographs. In addition to original fiction and books with favorite characters, there are Step into Reading Non-Fiction Readers, Phonics Readers and Boxed Sets, Sticker Readers, and Comic Readers—a complete literacy program with something to interest every child.

Learning to Read, Step by Step!

Ready to Read   Preschool–Kindergarten
• big type and easy words • rhyme and rhythm • picture clues
For children who know the alphabet and are eager to begin reading.

Reading with Help   Preschool–Grade 1
• basic vocabulary • short sentences • simple stories
For children who recognize familiar words and sound out new words with help.

Reading on Your Own   Grades 1–3
• engaging characters • easy-to-follow plots • popular topics
For children who are ready to read on their own.

Reading Paragraphs   Grades 2–3
• challenging vocabulary • short paragraphs • exciting stories
For newly independent readers who read simple sentences with confidence.

Ready for Chapters   Grades 2–4
• chapters • longer paragraphs • full-color art
For children who want to take the plunge into chapter books but still like colorful pictures.

STEP INTO READING® is designed to give every child a successful reading experience. The grade levels are only guides; children will progress through the steps at their own speed, developing confidence in their reading.

Remember, a lifetime love of reading starts with a single step!

For Jimmy, who won the game
—R.C.

CUPHEAD © and ™ 2022 StudioMDHR Entertainment Inc. THE CUPHEAD SHOW! ™
Based on the videogame from StudioMDHR.
Netflix™: Netflix, Inc. Used with permission.
All rights reserved. Published in the United States by Random House Children's Books,
a division of Penguin Random House LLC, 1745 Broadway, New York, NY 10019,
and in Canada by Penguin Random House Canada Limited, Toronto.
Step into Reading, Random House, and the Random House colophon
are registered trademarks of Penguin Random House LLC.
Visit us on the Web!
StepIntoReading.com
rhcbooks.com
Educators and librarians, for a variety of teaching tools, visit us at RHTeachersLibrarians.com
ISBN 978-0-593-43065-1 (trade)—ISBN 978-0-593-48531-6 (lib. bdg.)
ISBN 978-0-593-43066-8 (ebook)
Printed in the United States of America
10 9 8 7 6 5 4 3 2 1
Random House Children's Books supports the First Amendment and celebrates the right to read.

NETFLIX

THE CUPHEAD SHOW!

WELCOME TO THE INKWELL ISLES!

by Rachel Chlebowski

Random House 🏠 New York

Cuphead and Mugman are brothers.

They love cookies, adventure,

and each other.

Cuphead and Mugman

live in the Inkwell Isles.

Cuphead is confident and fun.

He is not always looking

for trouble . . .

. . . but trouble always seems
to find him—even in the
strangest places.

Mugman is more careful,

but he still loves exploring.

He is a good brother,
and he worries
about the trouble
Cuphead gets into.

9

Cuphead and Mugman
are very different.

Cuphead wears red shorts
and has a small red nose.

Mugman wears blue shorts
and has a big blue nose.

But both brothers have yellow
gloves on their hands and
big dreams in their hearts!

And both brothers would rather
go to a carnival than paint
a fence at home.

Cuphead and Mugman live with
Elder Kettle in his cottage.

Elder Kettle asks
the brothers to help
around the house.

He wants them to paint the white fence. He likes to keep them busy so they don't fight.

He hates it when they fight.

Cuphead and Mugman like

meeting people in the Inkwell Isles.

Ms. Chalice is a charming friend.

She has a spring in her step!

She's the best dancer

on the island.

Ms. Chalice is just as surprised as
Cuphead and Mugman when they
find trouble.

But they are
still friends.

Elder Kettle's house is close to Porkrind's store.

Porkrind sells all sorts
of things at his store,
but Cuphead and
Mugman love the toys
and games the most.

The Fly Trap is a boat club
in the Inkwell Isles.

It's owned by Ribby and Croaks,

a pair of brothers,

like Cuphead and Mugman!

Guests visit the Fly Trap

for fine dining—

and ice cream!

The Inkwell Isles are home to the good, the bad, and the in-between.

The Devil is definitely bad, and he's out to get Cuphead!

The Devil's deals
always sound like fun,
but they're also trouble.

Elder Kettle warned
the brothers to avoid
this kind of trouble!

25

King Dice is an entertainer.

He works for the Devil.

King Dice is full of tricks,

and not all of them are nice!

With suspicious characters like

King Dice and the Devil around,

Cuphead and Mugman

should beware of places like . . .

. . . the Carnevil!
Cuphead and Mugman
know better than to go
there, right?

LET'S GO!

Residents of the Inkwell Isles
have to be careful.
The Carnevil games are risky!

Will you be cautious,
like Mugman, or
daring, like Cuphead?

31

Cuphead and Mugman
are going to keep exploring . . .

. . . and finding trouble.
See you again soon!